T0194307

THE UNBORN

JONATHAN CALEB RUIZ

THE UNBORN

iUniverse books may be ordered through booksellers or by contacting:

iUniverse
1663 Liberty Drive
Bloomington, IN 47403
www.iuniverse.com
1-800-Authors (1-800-288-4677)

Because of the dynamic nature of the Internet, any web addresses or links contained in this book may have changed since publication and may no longer be valid. The views expressed in this work are solely those of the author and do not necessarily reflect the views of the publisher, and the publisher hereby disclaims any responsibility for them.

Any people depicted in stock imagery provided by Getty Images are models, and such images are being used for illustrative purposes only. Certain stock imagery © Getty Images.

ISBN: 978-1-6632-0380-9 (sc)
ISBN: 978-1-6632-0381-6 (e)

Print information available on the last page.

iUniverse rev. date: 06/24/2020

INTRODUCTION

I stand over a grave that I once cried over when I was small. The name reads, "Megan Anderson". She is the woman who raised me before her death. After she died, my whole world crashed around me when the demon in me woke up. I'm a broken warrior who is trying to overcome the evil in me. I must be stronger for my sake and for my loved ones. The woman who raised me said these words to me once, "Become someone stronger who even the demons would fear". Those words have been buried deep in my heart and mind. I want to escape, but the darkness follows me wherever I go. The only comfort I have is killing the cruel and evil people of this world. And then there's my everything, the woman who loves me, who sacrificed everything to save me and to be by my side forever. I must accept the darkness and become the devil itself. I must save the good and kind people of this world. I had people close to me who supported my struggles, family who always made me feel stronger when I'm scared or when I get lonely. These people have always known what has lived in me for the past six-teen years. They don't see me as a blood thirsty demon, ghoul, or evil person, but as a normal human who has a kind, noble, good personality and heart.

STORY

My story begins with the birth of me, a half-demon, half-human. After the day I was born, my father was murdered with his head cut off. After his death, me and my mother stayed together for seven years until that day. We had just finished shopping, so we went home. When we got there, men with katanas and guns were inside waiting for us. They claimed they were a part of the murder of my father. My mom yelled, then pulled a gun, and shot the leader in the eye. As he fell to the floor, he groaned and moaned. He quickly got up and yelled "Kill her and the kid!" My mother quickly wrapped her arms around me to shield me from the bullets. One by one, they shot her in the back. As she fell back, I cried in pain and rushed over her body. Her lasts words she told me was my dad's quote and "Embrace who you are, Jon." I screamed at them. One man approached me, he tries to grab me, but his hand gets cut off. I look up and see a strange man in front of me. He wore a cloth around his eyes, carried a knife on his hip, and a katana in both of his hands. He looks back at me and says, "Sorry I'm late, kid." He looks back at the men. One shoots at him, he deflects the bullet. He lunges forward with his blade, hits the man in the gut, then he moves his head towards the other men. He dashes at them and he kills three more. The others gasp and run out. The man with one eye runs out and says, "I'll see you around, kid." As I mourn over my dead mother, the man with the cloth approaches me and says "If you come with me, I'll teach you how to fight with your fists and weapons. I'll make you into a fine man someday. You will learn under me. I will guide you and teach you many things. If you come with me, I will be your master. I know everything about you, Jon. I'll help you master your powers to one day use it for good. What do you say, kid?"

Beginning

I reach out to him. He says, "You can call me your master. I will be by your side until I passed on my death." I cry in his arms and he pats my head to cheer me up. He takes me to a plane. We get in. Ever since I was smaller, I've heard voices in my head saying "Power, strength, kill, and blood." I didn't understand what he meant by "powers". I ask him before reaching out to him. I say to him "What powers are you talking about?" He looks at me, holds out his right hand to me, and says "You're the son of a devil." I look at him confused, but I was alone now. I was a kid who lost both of his parents. I reached out to him and he grabbed my hand. He picked me up and carried me in his arms while he started walking to the exit. As he walks me out in his arms. I glance back at my dead mother's body and saw that she was smiling when she died. My heart jumped out of my chest and it was trying to say "Bye mom. I will miss you. You're in my heart forever." I look at the man and I hold him close as the plane takes off. As I look out the window, he says, "I will take you back with me to Japan. That's where my home is. You have a Japanese last name that you inherited from your father. Your mother is American with a different last name. It seems that she wanted

you to have your fathers last name as a memory of his passing."
I look at him and say, "Thank you." I pause for a second and say,
"When will my lessons and teachings begin?" He looks at me
with a smile, then laughs, and says "We begin when we land."

New Life

As he had said, he took me to place I have never been before. He told me that Japan was his homeland, it's where he was raised his whole life. When we landed, he was talking to other people in a strange language. I am confused at what their saying. He looks down at me and says" Don't worry I'll teach you how to speak and understand the language." We look at each other and we let out a chuckle. We went to a mountain, and that's where his home was at. It was surrounded by nature not civilization. It was at a remote location, but it was nice and quiet. After I spend a day with him, he started teaching me his language and culture. I learned all of it in a year. Then he quickly taught me martial arts. I mastered it in three years. After that, he showed me how to craft a katana. I learned how to until I was fourteen years old. After I learned how, he put me to work on how to use a katana in a fight. For the next four years, I've been perfecting my blade skills. One day, I learned how to make katana blades. The first one I made was a small one, so I wrapped up and put it in safe keeping. The second blade I crafted was a regular blade. I showed the blade to my master. He first examined the outside of the blade, then he drew the blade out and practiced with it. He then said," It's a good blade for you. You must now name it to boost your skills and abilities. Since you have a demon in you, it will be your side. You must overcome it." As I head off to bed, I think about what master said. I think long and hard. Then it comes to my head. I decided to choose a name that's both perfect for me and the demon. I chose "Yurei Akuma", which mean Ghost Demon. When I fall deep in sleep, I dream of a place. It's dark and big. There's evil aura surrounding the area. I feel the pain, bloodshed, and sorrow of the place. I hear something come from behind me. I tilt my head backwards and a mist of black with red eyes is approaching me. I fully turn around and it is right in front of me. It smiles while looking evil and scary. I take a deep breath and it starts saying, "Hello, Jon. I'm your demon in you. My name is Yaokun. I appreciate you for accepting me in your mind. You are a demi-human after all." We both look at each other, then he takes out a weapon, and says "I like your weapon. I will be your blade. I will fight with you. When you need more power, you can always call my name and I will answer". I stare into his eyes and say, "We will fight together. But only if you promise that you won't take over my body or anything like that. You will be my weapon. Got it?" He looks at me, then lets a laugh, and says, "I understand fully. I am yours. I will be the weapon that you forged yourself and I will be your powers." I begin to disappear, and he says, "We'll see each other again." He waves at me and I wave back. He smiles, and I disappear to my world. Now, Yaokun talks to me when I train with my blade or when I am sleeping. We talk to each other when we get the chance to. I have been learning lots about him. He knew my father before he passed away. They both made an agreement that if my dad dies, Yaokun would be in my body as a sealed contract. So that is what had happened. I lost my father, but I gained a friend.

School Life

I turned sixteen last March when the Cherry Blossoms bloomed and fell to the Earth. One day, my Master came up to me with a uniform in his hand and with a smile on his face. He told me, "You will be going to High School from this day on." I look at him, then at the uniform. It's a blue top with a black bottom. I haven't been in school since Elementary. I skipped all Middle school. I do know Math, English, History, and Science from my Master. He taught me many things under him. I went off to bed, getting ready for my new school, and Master also prepared me for school. I wake up early, get ready, and begin to head off. Before I leave, Master stops me, hands me a note and sends his fair wells. The note that he gave me was for my homeroom teacher. All the faculty staff know that I was transferring in. A man who was by the gate asked me, "Are you the old man's kid?" I look at him, he is wearing a suit, and I nod at him. He lets a smile out and says, "I'm so happy that we will have you in our school. He told me that you were a foreign exchange student and that you have good grades." I nod, and he walks me to my class. He knocks, and a lady opens the door, steps out, and closes the door behind her. As they talk, I close my eyes and hear Yaokun's voice, "Have fun, my little darkness." I'm confused on what he said, but it made me glad that he cares for me like a guardian. They stop talking, the man leaves and waves bye to me. I wave back at him and lets out another smile. The lady says that she will be my new teacher. She says, "Are you ready for your new class?" I nod, and she opens the door. I get nervous and she walks in. "Okay students listen up. We have a new transfer student that will join our class today. He's a foreign exchange student. Jon, you can come in." I walk in and close the door behind me. I walk to the front besides the teacher. "You can introduce yourself," says the teacher. I take a deep breath, give them a little bow, and I say, "Hello everybody. My name is Jon Yukita. I'm from America. I was born there and when I was seven, I moved to Japan." They all examine me, and they begin asking questions. One asked, "How do you know Japanese?" I look at him, let a smile, and say, "A family member taught me." They clap a little. In the corner of my eye I caught something splendid. I see a beautiful girl with long crimson hair, who was staring at me. I turn to look at her. I smile at her and she blushes. Her cheeks turn red like her hair. She waves back at me. "She's so pretty," I say to myself. We smile to each other and I feel a strong connection with her. This is the first time that I will be with a large group of people that hardly know me, and I hardly know them. The teacher points to a desk next to the red-haired girl and says, "You will sit next to... Jon, are you okay?" I feel woozy and I close my eyes. The last thing I remember hearing, "Someone take him to the nurse!" I open my eyes up and I appear in Yaokun's realm once again. I look around and he is sitting down in a chair. I walk up to him and he says, "Take a seat, Jon." I sit down, and he gives me a serious look. He then begins to say, "There's a problem at your school." I respond, "What kind of problem?" He quickly says, "There is a devil at your school. I don't know how powerful he is. So, I want you to be cautious and careful." He still gives a look that he is worried. I know this is a serious problem because he is a devil himself. A demon afraid another demon. He says, "You must go now. You have to wake up and be careful." I feel something on my chest. I disappear from the realm. I begin to wake up and I slowly open my eyes. When I look at my chest, I see the girl from my class. The girl with the beautiful crimson hair. I look at her and say to myself, "Why is she here? Why is she sleeping on me? What happened after I pasted out?" I begin to shake her to wake up. She slowly opens her eyes. Then she looks up me and picks her head off my chest. She lets out a little yawn, then she barley realizes that she had used me as a pillow. She sits straight up and says, "I'm sorry for sleeping on you." I look at her and she has her head down low to hide her embarrassment. I say in my mind, "She is cute when she gets shy." I say to her, "It's alright." She looks at me with a confused look. "I thought you would be mad at me," she tells me. I let out a chuckle and tell her, "Why would I?" She looks at me and says, "You're not mad?" I tell her, "No, I'm not mad." She smiles and says, "Are you okay now?" I nod and tell her, "What happened after I pasted out?" She then tells me, "You have been out for two hours. The nurse asked for help, so I volunteered to help. I've been here since you pasted out." I tell her, "Thank you for being next to me all this time I've been out. I appreciate your help," I let out a smile. She blushes once again, smiles and says, "It's no problem." We sit there for a bit. She asks me, "You have a built body, Yukita. Were you in any sports before?" I responded with, "No I wasn't." She looks impressed and I tell her, "I'm sorry, I don't know your name." She gasps and says, "I'm sorry that I haven't introduced myself yet. My name is Kobayashi... Kobayashi, Sakura. Nice to meet you, Yukita." I remember that in Japan, people use your last name to talk to address you. I tell her, "You don't have to be so formal with me. You can call me Jon." She blushes, and says, "Nice to meet you... Jon. You may call me Sakura. Only if you want to." I smile and say, "Nice to meet you Sakura." We laugh together and the bell rings. "It's time for lunch. Let's head back to the classroom together," she says. She opens the door and the whole class looks at us. They all get in front of me and a boy says, "Are you okay, man? You were out quite a while." I tell him, "Yeah I'm good." A girl goes up to me and asks, "What happened? Why did you past out?" From the top of my head I tell them, "It's seems that I was tired. I stayed up late. I wanted my first day of school to go well." I let out a chuckle and they laugh. They day goes on. When the final bell rings, everyone heads to the front gate of the school. I head there myself. As I walk, I see three guys around a girl. In my mind I say, "Oh no... it's Sakura. The girl who was so nice to me. Those guys are causing trouble. "I must stop them", I say to myself. Strong preying on the weak." I walk closer and I hear the argument. The guys want her to go with them. She refuses, and one grabs her arm. She slaps him and pushes her down to the floor. He raises his fist at her. As he throws it her, she closes her eyes and is surprised to see me there. I caught his punch and he asked me, "Why are you interfering? This has nothing to do with you, new kid." I look at him and say, "Why? That's a funny question. Let me ask you something. Why are throwing a punch to a girl who is on the floor?" I put down his arm, he sighs, and I turn toward Sakura. "Are you okay, Sakura?" I ask her. I give her my hand, she reaches for it, and says, "Thanks to you, I'm okay now. Thank you, Jon." The guy yells out, "Ah, you take his hand but not mine. He's the new guy and you're already being all lovey dovely." She gets behind me and she holds my shirt. "It's clear to me that she's fears you and doesn't want to be with you. So back off. I don't want to do something that I'll regret later."

They begin laughing and he says, "What can you do against three people." I take in my Master's words, "Some people don't have powers like yours. Be a normal person. Don't hurt anybody, only if they have the urge to kill, then you can fight. Use self-defense only if they aren't a threat to you." I put my arm back and Sakura backs up. The guy in the middle tells his buddies to attack me. The first tries to punch me and I grab his arm and his buddy comes running. He kicks low to my stomach and I move out of the way. He knocks out his friend. He tries for another kick and he throws it high. I catch his leg and I throw him down to the ground. He falls, and the main guy stands in a martial art stance. He gets ready to strike and I let out a smile. He gets angry and says, "I will beat... beat you." He's surprised that I appear behind him during his sentence. He tries to strike backwards. I dodge, and I turn around. I see other students watching us and two adults run towards us. I stop, and I grab his arm that he threw at me. I put his arm to his chest and he lets his other fly at me. I dodge and let go of him. I tell him, "Turn around." He turns. There're students with their phones out and the teachers running to us. The teacher runs to me and one student yells out, "He didn't do anything. It was those three." As they point at them, they group up and the same man I met earlier was there. He walked up to those there. From their conversation, they were in the martial arts club. They walk up to me and the man says, "I'm sorry for these three causing you trouble." I nod and say, "It's no big deal. They were picking a fight that's all. I wanted to show them that weakness can be a strong suit for us who are not talented like them." He laughs, he takes them to the office, and he quickly says, "I will take responsibility for their actions. I'm their sensei after all." They leave and my body senses something strange about with those four. I leave it be and turn to Sakura. She looks relieved that she is not in trouble. I say to her, "You okay, Sakura?" She nods and says, "Yes. Thank you for saving me. That was amazing. You're so amazing." I laugh and say, "It was nothing special. My body moved on its own. I didn't want to see you get hurt." She blushes once again. She walks up to me and gives me a hug, "Well anyways, you were here to save me. My knight in shiny armor," she chuckles while telling me. She then says, "Can you walk me home? I don't want more trouble like that." I look at her, smile, and say, "Yeah. I'll walk you home. I can't leave you alone right now." She and I walked home together. We walked towards her home. She turned to me and asked me, "Why did you save me after all? I forgot to ask you that earlier."

LOVE?

I look at her, then I hold her, and tell her, "I hate to see the strong prey on the weak for their own pleasure and fun." She blushes, then she hugs me, and says, "Thank you. Are you free this Sunday?" She lets go and I look at her, then say "I don't have any plans. Why?" She smiles, and says, "Let us go somewhere together. Maybe at the mall. We can do some shopping." I think in my mind, "A girl asking a guy to go out with her. What did Master call this?" I ask her, "Is it just the two of us?" She blushes, and she has her hands together. "Yes. Oh… but it's not like that," she tells me while her face is red. "Like what?" I tell her. She looks up, then quickly says, "You know… when it's two people together…" I don't understand what she's is saying. I've never in my life have been out with a girl before. It's usually just me and Master shopping for things we need. I then tell her, "I'm sorry. I still don't understand what you mean by "Like that."" She looks up and says, "You really don't know what I mean?" I nod, and she talks again with her cheeks red, "When a guy and girl go out, it's called a… d-d-d-d-a--te." I look at her, she has her face towards the ground. I don't know what it means to love someone, especially a girl. I put my hand on her head, she looks up and I smile at her. I then tell her, "I have never been out a date before, it'll be my first time." She grabs my hand with both of her hands, and says, "It's a date then. Only if you want to. After all, I asked you out, so it's up to you. What you say?" I quickly respond, "Yes. Of course, I'll go out with you." Her face lights up and she says, "Yah. When I look into your eyes, I feel safe. I really enjoy being with you. I want to get to know you better, if you would let me?" We both stare into each other eyes and I feel something warm in my heart. It beats faster, and it aches. I don't know what love really is or what it means to love. I have never felt like this toward another person. She gives me a hug and says, "Let's hang out more at school. See you tomorrow. Good Night." I smile, wave, and say to her, "See you tomorrow. Let's talk more soon. Good night." She waves back and disappears into her home. I head home and get ready for the new day. The new day starts, and I head toward the station. Sakura is there waiting. She sits in the bench. She is looking down and call out to her. She hears me, stands up, and runs towards me. He gives me a big hug and says, "Good morning, Jon." "Good morning, Sakura," I say to her. We walk close together to school. People stare at us while and that guy who I "fought" is one of the people gazing upon us. He looks mad and he has a different vibe to him today. We enter the class and we sit in our seats. Me and her sit next to each other. Every day, we've been walking to school, eating lunch together, and talking lots more. One day, on Friday, we sat on a bench together and she asked me, "How did you happen to live in Japan?" I keep quiet and I look up at her. "My life wasn't all fun and games," I tell her. She gets closer to me and says, "What do you mean by that?" It's hard to her to tell her how my life came to be like this. I think if I tell, I will understand more about life, her and what love is. I have the courage to speak, and I say, "When I was born... my dad was murdered. Me and my mom were all alone.

She was the last family I had. I did not have brothers or sisters. My life was hard. I never met my real father. But then one day... my world crashed down right in front of me." She holds my arm and says, "You don't have to tell me if you don't want me to. If you do tell me, I will comfort you. I am here for you. I will bear your hardships with you." I look at her, she smiles, and I tell her, "My mom was killed right in front of me. We went shopping before my birthday and when we got back at our house... they were waiting for us. I can never forget that man's face. Scar on his cheek with only one eye." As I tell her, my eyes let out a little tear. When she sees me cry, she quickly wraps her arms around me. "It's okay. You can cry in my arms. I'm here." I remember those words "I'm here", my mother has always told me that she will be there for me. I cry in Sakura's arms and I wrap my arms around her. She puts her hands on my head and puts my head towards her chest. We sit for a bit. She comforts me. She's a sweet girl with a caring heart, but she has yet to know about me. We walk home together. She grabs my hand, and smiles. She is trying hard to be there for me. I feel grateful that I have meet her. We are at her house and before she goes in, she runs to me. She is right in front of me, she gives me a big hug, and says, "I'll see you Sunday. Make sure you're not late. I texted you the time and place where we are meeting at." She runs inside and waves at me. I head home. As I do, I feel something strange. I look around, and nothing is there. It feels like someone or something is watching me. As I walk, my heart hurts on the way to my house. I don't know what this means. "Am I really stupid when it comes to girls?" I keep telling myself what it means to love or to be in love. When I reach my home, Master is waiting outside, he sits on the floor, and he gets up to greet me. We get inside, and we sit down right across from each other. He tells me, "How was school today? You were a little late today. Everything go well?" I nod and say, "I actually met a girl. My first day of school, we started talking after I saved her from some guys picking a fight." "You didn't use your powers to fight them?", he says with a serious face. I nod, and I tell him, "No, I didn't throw a punch. I dodged their attacks and countered them." He congrats me. "Master, can I ask you something? I tell him. He laughs, and says, "You don't need to call me Master anymore. Call me dad or whatever. Okay, now what is your question?" I nod, have my hands on my lap, then I tell him, "Do you know what love is, old man?" He lets out a chuckle, then says, "Old man, I like it. Love huh... It's when you want to be with that person forever. You care for them, you want to protect them, you would do anything for them, and you want to be by their side. Are we talking about that girl you met?" I nod. He smiles and says, "Tell me what's going on." I then say to him, "My heart aches when I'm around her. I told her a bit about my past, the death of my parents, and she was there for me. She comforted me and let me lean on her. She told me to cry on her and I did. I believe that I love her, but I do not know. She also asked me on a date, and I said yes. We are going this Sunday. Does she love me, and do I love her, old man? Please tell me." He gives me a nudge on my head, he smiles, and says "You have found yourself a keeper. It's up to the both of you to express your feelings to each other. What I can tell you is everything about a relationship and how to properly love someone." I nod, and he begins talking until bedtime. As I fall asleep, I think to myself, "I think I know what love is now. I do love her, and I want to be by her."

DATE AND CONFESSION

I get ready for the date, I dress in my black attire. I'm not really a flashy guy. Plain and simple. I head out the door and I look behind me. The old man waves at me and says, "Enjoy yourself. You deserve it. You need to be a normal high school student." I wave back at him and say, "Thank you, old man." I head to the station where we are meeting at. I'm there ten minutes before our time. I wait, and I look at my watch. She's late. I get worried about her. I use my hearing. I hear a guy talking to a girl, she is scared and sounds familiar. I head over there. I guessed right, it was a guy trying to hit on Sakura. I get in between them and face towards Sakura. She looks relieved and I tell her, "I got worried, so I came looking for you. You okay?" She nods with a smile and I hear behind me, "Huh? Who are you, little brat?" I hold Sakura's hand and say to him, "I'm her date!" He looks mad, turns around and says, "Ah man! Beauties these days already have someone. Your lucky man, but it's not the last time you'll see me. I'll take her away from you." He leaves, me and Sakura look at each other. "You okay, Sakura?" I tell her. She nods, then smiles, and says, "Yeah. Let our date begin." She runs towards the station with her hand holding mine. We get on the train. We sit close to each other. I look at her. She is very lovely. "I don't know if we have the same feelings towards each other?" I tell myself. She holds my arm and says, "So we are going to the mall. Try not to get lost. Hold onto me the whole way." I nod. We sit there and then the train comes to a stop. She gets up and pulls me. "Let's go!" she says. We get off, head towards the mall, and we walk around. We walk around clothing stores, video stores, and many other things. We first head into a video store. She goes to a section, it says, "Anime". She looks happy while she is browsing through the videos. I tell her, "What's all this?" She looks at me and says, "You don't know what Anime is?" I nod no. "They are shows with different genres, like romance, action, and many more. I personally love Anime." I look at her and she continues, "I have a great idea. Let us buy some and we can watch them together another time. It will be a promise between us." "Yeah, let's do that," I tell her. She grabs a few and we head to the register. We pay half for them and we head to the next store. We enter a clothing store. A lady greets us on the way in. "Do you want to try on some cloths, young lady?," she tells Sakura. I say to her, "Do you want to try some on? She is willing to help you." She nods, and the lady says, "Perfect, let us begin." She goes into the changing rooms and the lady gets different styles of clothing for Sakura to try on. She tries in total number of five pairs. She tries on shirts, pants, shorts, and a dress. She looks great in everything. I was waiting for her the next cloths that she was going to show me. I hear Sakura say, "Jon... tell me how it looks." She comes out in a very beautiful top and skirt. I look at her and I can't speak. She looks gorgeous. "How is it?" she tells me. "I walk up to her and say, "It looks great on you. I like it." She blushes, turns to the lady and says, "I'll get this one, please." The lady tells her to change and put it in the bag. After she changes back to her cloths, we head to the cash register. I grab her hand and say, "I'll pay for it." She says, "Are you sure? I can buy it." I pat her head and say, "It'll be a gift from me to you." She gives me a big hug and we walk to the cash register. The lady says, "How sweet! Buying a gift for you girlfriend, young man." She smiles, then Sakura stops me from talking and she says, "He's a good boyfriend. He's the best." They continue laughing and talking. After they finish talking, the lady then says, "Here you two. You deserve it." She hands us a bag, it says "Couple Gift." She says, "We were doing an event and you two are the first ones to come in. All couples who come in, get this prize." I open it. It's full of lotions, perfumes, and colognes. I bow and tell her, "Thank you, ma'am." We head towards the exit, she waves goodbye to us, and we head off to more looking around. We walk around more until nightfall. We decide to go home. We walk to Sakura's house and she holds my hand while we walk. She smiles, hums, and holds me tight close to her. When we walk, I feel like I can be by her until the end. My heart aches and moans. My heart wants to reach out and express my feelings to her. I don't know exactly how she feels about me. Does she feel pity for me? Or is she just a nice person? Does she love me? I must find out. We continue walking to the direction her house. We stop right outside the house and I see a woman waiting there. She waves at us, then I turn to Sakura, and see her blushing. "It's my mom," she says. Her mom walks to us and Sakura is holding my hand. Her mom looks at me and she says, "You must be Jon. I've heard so much about you. I'm Sakura's mother. It's a pleasure to meet you." I bow and say, "It's nice to meet you Mrs. Kobayashi." She smiles at me and says to us, "I'll wait inside Sakura. I will leave now." She leaves, and Sakura looks down to the floor. I lift her head up and she's in tears. "I'm sorry Jon. I told my parents and my friends at school that we were dating already. I fell in love with you when we first met. The day you transferred to my school and class. When I first saw, I thought you were the one for me. I have never fallen in love before like this. I knew that you would have a kind-hearted personality. I wanted to be with you. Are you upset at me?" I look at her, then smile and say, "I'm not upset. I don't really know what to say. I'm happy that you like me and think as me like that, but…" Her face sinks to the floor. "I thought a guy was supposed to express their feelings first." She looks up at me with a smile on her face. "Do you want to be my girlfriend for real now?" She stops her crying, gives me a hug, and says, "I thought I was already." She chuckles and gives me an adorable smile. My heart feels for her. It wants to show her how much I care for her. I want to do something, but I don't know what to do. Then she tells me, "Jon, can you close your eyes?" she asks me while she blushes and her hands on my cheek. I do what she says and I wait. I feel a warm touch on my lips. "What is this?", I tell myself. I open my eyes quickly and her lips are pressed against mine. After she's done, she blushes and I tell her, "What was that?" She puts her hands on her face, uncovers her face, and says, "Was that your first kiss?" I nod and say, "Yes. Was that your first as well?" She nods and says, "Yes, it was." I am someone who is trying to understand what love is and that's what my main goal with Sakura. All I know is that I must protect her innocent smile. I have to be with her, for my sake and for hers, and for my… feelings. I must be her blade that she can trust her life on. I care deeply for her. As she departs into her home. She waves at me and I head home.

TRUTH UNFOLDING

As I walk down the street into the trail that leads to where I need to my home. I feel a dark presence around me. I look around me and I see someone standing on the cables near the street. He is wearing a mask to hide himself. I notice a mark on the mask that reminds me of something. As I think… I remember, it's the man who killed my parents, he had the same mark on his arm. The masked villain begins to speak, "Are my eyes deceiving me? A demi-human and human in love? This is too good to be true." He chuckles, "Do you know who I am?". I tell him no and he lets out a sigh. "Allow me to introduce myself to the previous Demon King's son. My name is Cynsharad, a demon servant, I am a demon who follows the two great demons who will destroy this world and you." I look at him, and say "No way I'm going to let that happen! I know you go to my school and you are spying on me." He claps, then he begins to disappear, then says "Congrats on knowing that information, but you will soon meet the same fate as your father. You're the only one standing in my master's way to world domination. Heed my warning, within the next three days, we will begin our attack. All three of us will take this world to hell." He disappears and I begin running home. I get there and I tell the old man of what has happened. He begins thinking about what he is going to do. I suddenly get an ache in my heart and I remember about Sakura. I quickly turn to my master and say, "Old man?" He looks at me and asks, "What has happened?" I tell him, "Can I tell Sakura who I really am? I believe she need to know." He thinks about it, closes his eyes and opens them after a few seconds. "Go ahead and tell her. When you do, remember that if she gets scared of you, don't force her to accept you." "She wont sir, she cares for me and I care for her enough for myself to be her shield," I say to him. I grab my phone and call Sakura. The phone rings, then I pick it up. I hear, "Hello Jon. Why did you call me so late?" I respond, "I need to talk to you. It's about me." She says, "Yeah, okay. Meet me tomorrow at the train station before school. Don't be late, okay? Bye Jon." As I hang up the phone, I feel at ease that I can get the fear out of me. I can talk to somebody about what slumbers within me and who I am. My whole life up to now has been really unfair and horrible. I'm a descendant of a devil king, my parents were murdered, and I've been training almost my whole life. Now, I have someone who I love and care about. I will tell her who I am and what will happen between us if things like this continues to move forward. As I fall asleep, I get more and more anxious about how Sakura take my news. My heart needs to be prepared if she doesn't accept who I am. I re-act scenes in my head on how the conversation will end. I try not to stress about it, so I decide to just sleep. As the day comes, I leave with regret and pain that I will be forgotten by her. I meet up with her and she greets me with a big smile on her face. "You wanted to talk, Jon? What is it about?" She says with a cute grin on her face. I say, "Can we talk somewhere more private?" She nods, takes my hand, squeezes it, and pulls me with her. She leads me to a park and we sit on the nearest bench. Then she says, "So what's up? You can tell me anything. I care for you. And...well...I...Love You!" When I hear her words, my heart bursts with excitement and I get the courage to tell her. "I love you, too." As I say, she looks at me all flustered, and says, "Was that all you needed to tell me or is there more?" I look at her and tell her, "There's more." I take a deep breath and I begin talking, "No that much people know this about me, but... I am not completely human." She looks at me with confusion, "What do you mean?" she says. I stand up with my left arm on my side and my right in the air. I say, "Come forth, Yurei Akuma!" My blade appears before us and she has a surprised expression on her face. "You're a magical human!" as she claps. "No that's not it. Look, let me show you," as I tell her. I put the sharp end of my blade on my left wrist. She looks at what I am doing, "What are you going--?" As she tries to finish her sentence. I slice my wrist and blood pours out. She quickly gets up, holds my blade down and grabs my bloody wrist. "Why did you do that? You can get an internal bleeding damage from cutting yourself like... that?" She stops to see a little light catch her attention and she looks at my cut. It's gone and she examines the wound. "This is what I mean. I'm not magical nor a one-hundred percent human. I am a Demi-Human with powers." I take a pause to see what she says. "I am so sorry for not telling you sooner. I thought you wouldn't accept who I truly was." She puts her head down and I hear a "sigh" come from her. I look at her and she lifts her head up with a sad- cute-mad face. She has her mouth like a fish and her cheeks together like a little baby. She then calms down and begins talking, "I would accept you no matter what you are or what you do. That's what love is. I care for you so much that if you were in trouble that I would go save you in a heartbeat. I don't want you to think that I don't care about you, because I do. So very much that I would die for you. Remember that!" She holds my cheeks in her hands and kisses me. After the kiss, I hold her in my arms and say "I am sorry for my idiocy and arrogance. I love you so much. Would you forgive me by staying with me?" She sighs again, "I already told you that I would stay with you no matter what happens." She lets out an adorable smile. I feel relieved that I hear her say those words, "Wow. I'm dating a devil. It's exciting," she says. "Well I'm a half demon," I correct her. "Well either way, it's fun dating someone who is different from you." She continues talking and we walk out of the park. We hold hands and she start to cling onto my arm. As we walk, "I got an idea, Jon." She says with a bright expression on her face lighting up. I nod and she whispers into my ear, "Let's skip school today. Let's go on a date today?" I nod yes. She lets out a cute "Yes".

TRUE SELF

We walk around the shopping district. We head into many different places. We went into an arcade, shoe store, clothing stare, and a...fun place? The place had a swimming resort, another arcade, refreshments area, and a sports center. We decide to go to the pool. We rent out some swim suits. I put the trunks on and leave my white shirt on. I head out and I see lots of people there: little kids, young adults, and middle-aged people. I walk towards Sakura's changing room and she is there waiting for me. She runs to me and lets a smile out. "Why are you in a shirt? Your seeing me in a bikini right now. By the way, how do I look?" I look at her and I tell her, "You look lovely and adorable." She smiles and she continues to question me about my shirt. She puts her hands on my shirt. She pulls it up and I stop her. "I don't think it's a good idea," I tell her. "Don't worry. Look at all these people. They are just fine. Take it off." I give in to her request and I decide to let her undress my shirt. She pulls my shirt up and I hear her gasps. She looks at my body from the front and the back. "Wow. You have a nice body," she tells me. "You don't mind the scars that I have?" She nods and I turn behind me. I see girls looking at me, some wave at me, and some come over to me. They look

25

at my body and ask me questions. "What happened to your body? Or "Are you seeing somebody?" I tell them that I was in harsh training and that I've been training since I was small. They get closer to me. A hand pulls me and it's Sakura. The girls yell, "Who are you?" Sakura tells them, "I'm his girlfriend." They turn to me and I nod. "It's true. We love each other. But thank you ladies for asking me these questions." They turn and leave. Sakura holds onto me, pulls me away, and says, "Don't ever do that to me. It hurts me when you talk to other girls. Okay? Your mine and mine alone." Her expression changed and she is upset. I hold my arms to her, she goes to my arms and I tell her, "I'm sorry for hurting you. I love you. I am yours and yours alone." Those words change her expression. She is happy and is hugging me tight as I was a stuffed toy. "Your holding me too tight, Sakura," I tell her. She lets go and she is blushing, "I'm sorry. Your just so soft. You're like a teddy bear. Your skin is so soft and delicate." I hear her and my face turns red. She looks at me and holds my face with her hands. "You look really cute right now with your embarrassed face." She kisses me, we walk together and decide to have fun. We swim, play and talk in the water. We splash around. We have fun for the next hour and we decide to leave. As we walk towards the changing rooms, these two men approach us. "Hey girl. Care to hang with us? You can ditch this loser," one tells, while the other is giggling the whole time. She goes behind my back, puts her arms around my chest and hugs me. When she does, I feel her breasts press against my back and I get this nice sensation from that. I get embarrassed and I turn red. "Sakura?" I ask her. "Don't hold me too tight." She lets go a little, but I can still feel them press against me. The two guys look at with disgust and one says, "Don't you dare try to mock us, you nobody." Then Sakura says, "Well this nobody is my boyfriend and he is mine. He is always there for me." When I hear her speak of good, my heart jumped out and gave her a big hug. The bigger guy tries to grab Sakura from behind me and I snatch his hand before he could. I bend it and flip him on his bottom. He looks surprised and he orders his friend to get me. He quickly gets up and they both dash towards me. The smaller guy tries to pull a punch, but he stops in place gazing into my eyes. I showed him my demon eyes and he goes straight to the floor. When my eyes turn red, I can put someone into sleep when they look into them. As he falls, the other pulls a punch and I back up. As he swings, he stumbles and falls into the pool. I turn around and look at Sakura, "Sorry about that. You should head into the changing room." She walks into the room and I head into the men's dressing room. As we finish, we meet at the exit of the place. I wait for her and she comes out. She comes running towards me with her arms up high. She hooks around me with her arms and gives me a big squeeze. She holds me tight and says, "Thank you, darling. I love you." I look at her and ask her, "Darling? What's that?" She holds my hand and says, "It's a couple name for you, like a cute name for me to call you. You can make one up for me, if you want?" I nod, then I think, something that I can call her. I blurt out to her, "What about... little fox? It's cute and it has red fur." She nods and says, "I like it. I'm happy that you can of me as a cute fox." She lets out a cute giggle. We walk out and head to more stores. I hear a roar. The sky turns black and it starts to rain. We go into a store and we stay there for a bit. "I can't believe it," Sakura says with frustration. "We were having a good date and now this happens." I hold her head towards my chest and she puts one arm around me. I give her my jacket and tell her, "You want to go to my house for a bit?" She looks up at me with sparkles in her eyes and says, "Yes!" We walk towards my house, when we hear a "roar". The sky turns blacker and she pulls me when she begins running towards the path. We run to my home before it starts to pour more. We get there and the old man is waiting on the porch. He greets us and gives us a big smile. He tells us to change out of our clothes and take a shower. I lead Sakura into the bathroom for her to change. I give her a towel and an extra pair of clothes. I walk into my room and the old man follows me. "Jon?" I turn around and he hands me a box. He tells me to open it. As I open it, I get the feeling that I've seen this box somewhere before. I look inside and it's a small blade, it's about three inches high and two inches thick. I look on the side of the blade. "Jon Yukita". It's the first blade I made when I first came into this country. "Now, you can give your treasure to the one you love. Protect her and cherish her." I give him a hug and tell him, "She accepted who I was. She did not care for who I am. But the person I am now." I let go and he says, "I know she accepted you. I looked into her eyes." After he talks to me, he steps out and Sakura walks in. "Wow. Sorry… this is my first time in a guys room." She says while blushing. "Yeah. It's not too flashy. I like to keep it simple. I have my books, swords, and other stuff in the dojo next door." I hold the box in my hand and she looks at it. "What's that?" She says while sitting on my bed. I sit next to her and I hand her the box. "It's for you." She opens it and she looks inside. "It's the first blade I made when I was smaller. I want you to keep it. I want you to protect yourself just in case if I'm not there." She lets out a tear and quickly wraps her arms around me with her head on my chest. "Thank you. I swear I shall repay the favor and save you sometime. I love you with all my heart. I want to be with you forever." She leans towards my face, plucks her lips together and closes her eyes. She kisses me and I close my eyes. This warmness is something I can never forget and I will always love. "Knock- Knock". I open my eyes and the old man is by the door. "I'm sorry to interrupt, love birds." Sakura quickly goes back. Her face turns red and she puts her hands on her face. "Hi there, Jon's dad," Sakura says. The old man laughs and says, "Don't mind me." We laugh and he says, "What has Jon told you, Sakura?" She looks up on him. She says, "Well he told me he was not all human, but a demi- human." He looks at me and says, "That's all you told her." I nod and Sakura looks at us. "What else is there? She says. The old man says, "It first started when Jon was born into this world." She looks at me, grabs my hand, and holds tight. "When he was born, his father was killed. His father was a demon king. Jon and his mother were left all alone. She supported the both of them throughout his life. He was seven when his mother was also killed. She was killed by the same men who killed his father. Jon was their target and they wanted to rid of the royal bloodline. His mother protected him long enough for me to kill those devils who wanted the power to themselves. They were selfish beings who wanted the throne for their master. Now, we face a threat." Sakura looks at me and asks, "What threat?" He inhales and exhales, "The new king and his minions are coming. Jon met one who was hiding in your school. The man with one eye who killed his mother. He is the general of the demons along his new king." I look down and Sakura puts her chest on the top of my head. "He is their target, so he must be ready to defend this world, protect all life, and kill the demon invaders. The world is in his hands." I raise my head to Sakura's eyes, lean my head to her chest and I give her a big hug. "I love you," I whisper into Sakura's ear. She looks at me with a devastating stare in her eyes. "I don't want you to die, so please come back alive after the fight," she tells me. After a few minutes of talking, me and Sakura leave. I walk her to her house and we say goodnight to each other.

BATTLE

The next day starts and we go through the same routine. I get up early and head to Sakura's house to pick her up. As I walk to her home. I sense something wrong and I look around. I see nothing but the alley I'm walking through and the light pole that is standing in the side as a spectator. As I calm down, my phone buzzes. I get it out and it's a text from Sakura. "I woke up early today, so I'm waiting at the train station. See you later, Darling!" "Darling?" I whisper with a smile. I head to the station. As I walk, I feel a dark presence, I look around and nothings there. I decide not to worry about it and I continue towards the station. I see a girl stand near a post with a pink skirt, a blue shirt, wearing a cap with beautiful red hair. That's her, the Sakura I know and care about. She sees me, dashes to me, and wraps her arms around me like a kid getting a teddy bear for a present. She squeezes me, grabs my hand and she leads me towards a shopping district. We walk around and I see something that catches my attention. "Hōseki." "Is that Jewelry?" I whisper under my breath. We walk more ahead and we head into a store. Sakura shops around a clothing store and she tries on clothing in the fitting room. As she does, I disappear outside. When I return, I hear my name. I walk towards the sound and its Sakura. "Jon. Tell me what you think about this dress." She opens the curtain slowly and she steps out. As my eyes gaze upon the dress, my heart beats, and my eyes shine. She wears a beautiful pink short dress. Her face turns red and she asks, "What do you think?" I walk closer to her lean towards her and say, "You look amazing. That dress suits you." She puts on her left hand on her cheek and the other on my chest, "Thank you," she says. She gets closer to give me a kiss, but she stops after we hear, "Kobayashi?" She turns red and looks at whom called her. It was a girl with scar on her right cheek. I have never seen her before, but she examines me and goes to Sakura. She hugs her and asks, "Who's this?" as she points to me. Sakura responds, "He's my boyfriend." She lets out a chuckle, walks to me, and lets out a small hit on my chest. "You better take care of her, kid," she says. She was a little shorter than me, but she called me a kid. I was confused. Then Sakura says, "She's my aunt." I look at her and she lets out a smile. I say "It's nice to meet you, ma'am. My name in Yukita Jon." "Nice to meet you, Jon," she responds. I look at her scar and ask, "What happened? How did you get that scar?" She looks at me, points to her cheek, and says, "Oh this. It was a stupid thug with an eyepatch. He just cut my face after I told him to stop being a bad person when we was robbing a bank." I take in that word... eyepatch. A man with one eye. I ask her, "Did you notice any other marks or symbols?" She looks at me and slowly says, "Y- yes, I did. Do you know who it was?" "I might know who it is. Where was the mark at?" I ask her. She responds, "On his arm. How do you know this man?" I whisper under my breath, "It's him. He's the second devil." Then, I look at her and say, "Thank you." She nods and I walk off. Sakura finished changing, but before she leaves, she talks to her aunt. I listen in. "Is he okay," Sakura's aunt asks. "It might be the person who killed his parents. That's why he's like that right now. Anyways see you later," Sakura tells her. I continue walking and I hear my name. I turn around and it's Sakura running to me. She gets stopped by three men who are blocking her path towards me. She gets scared and falls back. I walk behind the men. One man says, "Sorry about that missy. Would you care to come with us to repay you for your troubles?" They all let out a chuckle. She begins to shed tears and she is scared. I grab one man by the shoulder and say, "Did you just make my girlfriend cry?" They all turn to me and the man tries to brush my hand off of him. My hand locks in and flips him on his side. The other says, "We'll make you pay, brat. How dare you hurt one of ours." They take out weapons. One knife and one katana. The first lunges his knife at me and I grab the blade out of his hand. I throw it to the ground and I put him to sleep. The last one stays still and he says, "I'll kill you." I put my right leg back and I dash towards him. I appear behind him and he slowly turns. Eyes red, black hair and no expression on my face. He gets scared and tries to swing at me. I hit him in his chest with my palm, he lets out a moan, and stumbles backwards. I walk towards him, place on finger on his chest, and push him. He falls backwards on his back. I quickly walk to Sakura. She stops crying and she tries to get up. She lets out, "Ow. My ankle hurts. I think I sprained when I fell." She holds a bag in her hand and her tries again to get up. I catch her before she falls. "What did you get?" I tell her. "I got the pink dress. The one you liked," she responds. I grab my arm on her legs and my other under her head. I carry her like a princess. "What are you doing?" She asks with a red face. "You hurt your foot, so I decided that I'll carry you home." She nods and I walk out to the district towards her home. People look at us as I walk. She blushes and hides her face from the people. We get to this street with nobody, but I feel something. Something feels wrong... like someone is watching us.

Enemies Appear

I continue to walk out of the street. I get a bad feeling and I set down Sakura. "What's the matter, Jon?" she asks me. I grab a pebble and toss it in front of us. It bounces back. "I knew it," I say. "Jon, what's going on?" Sakura asks. I respond, "It seems they started their attack. We got caught in a trap." Laughter echoes through the street. The man in the mask appears, Cynsharad. He is joined by two other man. One looks familiar and the other is someone who I haven't met. I see an eyepatch on the second man, and my head begins aching. "It's him... The one who murdered my parents," I whisper to myself, but Sakura heard me. "Jon? Are you okay," she asks me. I hold both hands in a fist. I feel a warm and soft hand hold onto my clutch fists. I look to my right and she has a worried look on her face. I calm down, I take a deep breath and I smile at Sakura. I walk in front of her and give her a pat on her head. She smiles back at me and I stand in front of her with my back facing her. "So, you're the devils who have come to kill me, then when I'm dead, the world will be yours," I yell at them. The third laughs, and says, "You're a clever boy. You are really are "his" son." "You knew my father before your friend over killed him?" I ask him. He lets out a chuckle, "Yes, in a matter of fact he was my lord. I was a general in the army and he was our king. Zamorok, the shadow of darkness, is the name of your father, Jon!" "NOW, I am the king. The one right to the heir. You are the only one who is a threat to our seeking of world domination. We must kill you in order to purge this world." I let out a giggle. "Huh? What's so funny kid?" he asks me. "Oh, it's noting," I respond. "What's your names? I already met Cynsharad over there." Cynsharad takes off his mask. It's the kid who tried to hurt Sakura on my first day of school. "You knew who I was the whole time?" he asks me, while he points at me. I nod, "I knew ever since we first fought and when you were spying on me, you gave off the same presence." They all clap and I take a step back. "Now," as I point to the man with the eyepatch, "You must be the one from back then. The one who murdered my mother right in front of me…" He bows and says, "That's me. The one and only, Ardame. The one who commands the underworld." I get down on one knee next to Sakura. "Lastly, it's my introduction. I am the new Demon King, Barbas. The one who killed your father with his bare hands," as he holds his hands up to sky as he laughs. "Now let's begin the extermination of you and your girlfriend!" as says while he orders the two to attack while he stays back. I stand up as they walk slowly to us. I call out "Yurei Akuma". Lights appear in right hand. I reach to my left hip and pull out the blade with my right hand. They stop and pull out their weapons.

WAR

They both come at me and I walk to them. Cynsharad swings at me and I block it. Then, Ardame swings to my side and I pull out a kunai to block his attack. "Now," as I get in a defensive stance, I speak to them both, "Come at me!" Cynsharad dashes over to me and his swing is high. I put my right leg back, use my blade on my right hand to block and use the kunai in my left hand to slice his sword in half. His sword breaks in two and he "gasps." He steps back and still runs at me. I grab my blade with two hands and whisper, "Sha No Kuma." He gets within range and I strike at him, but Ardame stops my blade. They both jump back. "That strike was a killing blow. If I wasn't there, your head would've been clean off," he tells to Cynsharad. "Take out your demon weapon. He is using a forged katana. It's strong and deadly. It has the aura as his father's." They both call out and take out blades from the ground. Ardame is using a sword, while Cynsharad uses a bow. He shoots at me, but I dodge. I pick up Sakura and bring her to safety. Ardame chases us and he strikes at us. I block it, but we get launched back. As we fall, we get caught by a demon spell. I look around and the devils are looking behind us. I look in the direction and see a shadow enter the field. It's my master, the old man has come to save us. "I knew they would attack early. Sorry I got her late," he says. The old man catches me in the air and we land safely to the ground. "I had it under control," I tell him with a smile. I walk back and set down Sakura. "Stay here and be safe," I tell her. "I'm sure you had it, but it seemed you needed a hand," the old man tells me. "Now," as he looks at the two demons, "Let us get back to it." "Yeah let's," I say to him. I make a fist towards my master and say, "Let's do this." He bumps it and we walk towards them. Ardame smiles and yells, "It's been a while old man. Still got that cloth around your eyes? Your mine, I will kill you this time." The old man smiles and says, "I see you got that loud mouth of yours." I laugh. Ardame yells, then runs to us, and yells to Cynsharad, "Cover me." He swings at the old man fast, but he catches the blade in the air before it hits him. He pushes him back and he falls. He stands up, and continues to strike the old man. As I try to move towards Cynsharad. Ardame chants and appears behind me. He swings down upon my back, I turn around, and block it. The force pushes me back. I stand up and I quickly turn to Cynsharad. He stabs me with a dagger in my stomach. I fall slowly to the ground. Ardame jumps up and strikes down to me. His blade pierces my shoulder. I kick him off with little of my strength, as I do, I gaze at the dark sky. As I lay there, I hear clashing of weapons, arrows flying, and my name. "JON!" I roll over to my belly and lift my head up. I see Sakura crying. The old man is fighting both of them. My wounds begin to heal slowly. I slowly get up. Another arrow flies to me. It hits my leg, and I fall back down. I get back up, pull the dagger and arrow from my body. Blood gushes out. Ardame notices that I have not been killed. He changes his target to me. I block his first attack and my katana flies in the air besides me. He then takes his sword and lunges it to my gut. He puts it all the way in, where the hilt is touching my body. The old man kicks Ardame off and he flies towards Cynsharad. Ardame laughs, pulls another blade from the ground, and says, "Your still not dead yet?" as he holds up the blade behind his neck, "Your powers are really something. After we kill you. We will take that power from you." The old man takes the blade from within my stomach and throws it away. Ardame lunges to me. I fall back and the old man is up to his face. It's back to him protecting me again… over and over. I hate to feel worthless. I wish I had more "power." Then I hear a voice in my head. "I think it's time for you to unlock your full potential, Jon. What do you think?" The voice is familiar. Yaokun has finally showed up. "Grab your blade and repeat this chant," he says to me. I crawl to my katana. I grab the blade part and my hand bleeds. I hear the words and I begin repeating them while on my knees. "I am the heavenly demon who seeks punishment and execution of those who seek to destroy my world and the people of this world. I protect the innocent and reap the guilty. I MUST PROTECT MY LOVED ONES." My body aches and I scream. "Ahh." My scream turned the faces to those around me. "What's going on?" Barbas asks. My legs stand up and my face is looking into the sky. As I regain conscious, I look at the faces of the enemies. They have a surprised expression. I look down to my blade. It looks sharper, blacker, and has an aura around it. "Your powers have awakened, all of it," Yaokun says. He laughs and says, "Let's put an end to these worthless devils." Words come to my head from Yaokun. I repeat them. I appear behind Cynsharad and slash at him. He blocks it with his bow and it breaks in half. "How are you stronger and why are your eyes red and blue. I look into my blade. I see my right eye is red and my left is blue. I smirk at him and lunge to him. Ardame blocks my attack, but gets pushed back. He quickly gets up and tries again at me. I block and the old man helps out. He dashes to Ardame. He swings at him, but Ardame dodges, and strikes my master. I turn my eyes to the old man as he gets sliced on his arm and flies back to me. I quickly catch him before he hits the floor. "Thanks, Jon," he tells me. "What lovely eyes you have. Their like gems." I set him down and I say, "Will you be okay?" He nods and says, "Close your eyes and lower your head." I comply and as he says. I feel a warm touch on my forehead. "Release," I hear from my old man. I feel a lock opening within my heart. A gust of winds surrounds me and the old man. "When you were born, your father locked your powers that he passed down to you. I am the only one who knew about it and who has the key for it. He trusted his powers to you when you were ready and could handle the pain." He closes his eyes, "Let me rest for a bit. I trust that you can handle this yourself." I nod to him. I pick him up and carry him to Sakura. I set him down besides Sakura. "Take care of him for me," as I look at her with a smile. "I will. Win this battle and be safe," she tells me. I nod and I turn to the enemies. I walk and Ardame lunges at me. I block it with my bare hands. I push him back and he goes through the air towards Barbas. He falls down onto his back. "How interesting! Your now even more powerful. Defeat these two if you can and face your final boss," Barbas yells out. Cynsharad looks at Barbas, "Sorry my lord. I know this is taking a while to…" as he tells him, as he looks at me disappear. His face is surprised and worried. He looks around for me. As Ardame slowly gets up on his feet. I appear behind Cynsharad and strike his stomach. He falls to the ground and lets out a moan. "How- how did you get behind me that silently?" he asks me while in pain. "I used the shadows to get there. I am the son of the previous demon king," I tell him. Ardame yells, "Not my student!" I look at him while I cut off Cynsharad's head off. His body falls down and his head rolls to my feet. I grab his hair and lift it up. I face it towards Ardame. He yells and dashes with anger at me. He strikes at me, but I dodge and throw the head at him. He drops his sword and catches it. I teleport in front of him. I lunge my tip of my blade into his eye. It pops and his eye starts bleeding. He starts swinging punches at me. His arms are swinging at different directions. I grab his neck from behind. He starts scratching at my face. I put my arm around it and squeeze. I hear a crackle sound and he falls down to the ground faced forward. He drops the head as he falls. "Two down. Now it's Barbas who is left," I say to myself. I turn my head to Barbas, and say, "It's your turn to die de--."

FINAL STAND

As I am about to finish my sentence, a blade insets my back, I turn around, and see Barbas standing behind me. I fall to my knees. He laughs and says, "Those two were far weaker than me." I groan and blood squirts out as I pull the blade from my back. "Look on the bright side, you did avenge a dead family member that was murdered. But… you were never kill me. I have many powers. I will be even stronger after I take your powers from you. I will even kill GOD!" he tells me while he starts to begin laughing. "Now it's your turn to reunite with your parents and soon will you little girlfriend. She will go with you as well after I finish with you. So long JON!" he yells while he raises his blade to my head. I sit there to await my fate; I close my eyes and take a breath. I hear, "Don't worry, Jon. I'm here to protect you this time. I love you." I open my eyes, I see Barbas start to lower his blade to me until I see blood come out of his mouth and chest. It's Sakura who stabbed him. She looks at me with a smile and says, "I told you it was my turn to protect you." She lets go of the blade into him, Barbas turns to her and lunges to her. "You DAMN human!" he yells. He grabs her arm and the blade goes into her stomach. He takes out the blade and blood comes out of her. My face is surprised and I reach out to her. I quickly catch her before she hits the ground. She falls into my arms. Barbas jumps back and struggles to pull out the blade from his back. He groans and moans. "Why does a blade like that hurt so much," he yells. As he struggles, I look at Sakura. I shed a tear. She puts her hand on my cheek and says, "I'm glad I got to protect you as least one time. Your wounds have healed... so-so fin---fin-finish this." She closes her eyes and her hand falls to the ground. I scream and moan. "NO. Please not you. Sakura wake up. Don't leave me alone. I LOVE YOU." I cry and pout. As I look at her face, I look at her lips. I lean down and kiss her. Blood drips into her mouth and her lips still feel warm. Blood... just like her hair... that's the color of the hair that I loved. The one who loved and cared for me. Beautiful crimson hair at my hands. "I'm sorry Sakura. I'll make this right," I say to her as I stand up. "Finally got this stupid knife out," Barbas says. He then looks at me, and grins wide. "Did she die? Stupid girl should've stayed away from this fight. Did her death hurt you, did it change you? Are you STRONGER," he says to me. He continues laughing evilly. I look down, and take a deep breath. Anger flows through my body, takes over every inch of my soul and spirit. A change happens to my body, I don't know what it might be. I look into the reflection of my blade and I see white hair. Anger controlled me and has changed my hair. I grin, look at Barbas in the eyes, and get in my stance. He smiles, "You have got stronger, oh how this is delightful. I get to use the full strength of my power." He gets out a red katana from the ground. "This the great demon katana. It will take your life and purge this world down to ashes." He gets in a stance. I get in position myself. "I will end this in one strike!" he yells. "Let's end this quick, shall we. I plan to kill you with my vengeance." I hold my blade with both hands close my eyes. "Pour everything into my blade. Hatred and vengeance."

We take off to each other. We appear behind each other. Barbas drops to the ground, he groans and blood pours out of him. "What the—what happened?!" he says. "My techniques are far better than yours. This is for everything you did to me. You're going to die now," I tell him. I hold the blade high, "This is for my loved ones." I strike down and I decapitate his head. His body and the other bodies disappear along with him. The barrier goes down, and the night sky is covered in stars. I walk over to my master's body. He wakes and says, "I knew you could do it. You unlocked all your powers. Now you must go to her," as he points to Sakura's body. I walk to her body, I look back, and the old man starts walking to our house. I go down on both knees, hands on them, besides her body. I bow down and remember something. I reach into my pocket, and grab a small ring. I slide into her finger. I shed a tear, and pick her up. I start walking to her home. I must tell her parents what happened to her and who I am. I look up as I walk, close my eyes, and see all the fun moments I had with Sakura. When she's shy, cute, beautiful, kind, smart, lovely, and when's she mad, yelling my name and calling my name. As I think of the memories, I smile and hear my name once more in my head, or is it.

Epilogue

I open my eyes after I hear, "Jon? What happened to you." I slowly look down, and I gasp. I cry and drop to my knees. "Whoa. What's happening? What happened to my shirt? And what's up with your hair?" I stand back up; I smile at her. "Don't worry. We won. We're free," I tell her. I calm down and notice that my body has gone back to normal. She says, "Your eyes and hair are back to normal." I take a deep breath. "I'm glad I got to save you, but how am I still alive?" she asks. I think about it and I tell her, "When you died, I kissed your mouth, I must have transferred some of my blood into your system when I kissed you. I was bleeding when I kissed you." She smiles, she looks at her wound, it was all healed up. There was a scar where her wound was, and she noticed something shiny on her finger. She looks at it and examines it. She gasps, then looks at me, "This is beautiful. When did you--- You know what I'm not going to ask, but I love it." "When I got it, the lady told me if I had any special girl, I responded yes. Then she said that she has the ideal ring for someone who wants to stay with that person for a long time, so I got it for you, for that sole reason," I tell her. I take a deep breath, and say, "Will you stay with me forever?" She turns red,

43

the says, "Do you even know what your saying? Your asking me to be your wife, your family. This is a marriage proposal." I walk more until we reach her home. I set her down, I hold her hands. "I do want to be with you until death. I love you more than anything. I want you to be my wife," I tell her. She looks down and blushes hard. "Yes. I will be your wife. I love you more than anything." We both look at each other. We lean in close to each other, we kiss and our names are called. "Jon. Sakura. Sorry for interrupting." It's her mom. "You know. If Jon asked your hand in marriage, we would gladly say yes," she tells yes with a smile. Sakura shows her mom the ring and she gasps. "Is that what I think it is!" she says happily. "Yes, it is. Jon asked me to marry him just right now," she tell her mom. "Mrs. Kobayashi?" I say. She turns to me and says, "Yes?" "Will you let me marry your daughter?" I ask her. She quickly says, "Yes!" "You'll have to get married after finishing school, which is not far. I will do all the planning and we will pay for it," she tells us with a big smile on her face. She invites me in and I accept the invitation. I hold Sakura's hand and we walk inside.

END

As I open my eyes, I see the grave we stand on, me and Sakura, hand to hand. We get married in a month. We have done everything together ever since I asked for her hand in marriage. We have memories of our best and worst moments in our life. She has a scar now, for when she risked her life to save me from the devils who wanted world domination. She is my everything. I promised her that I wouldn't let anything else happen to her. I am no ordinary human, she accepted me, and chose to fall in love with me. Now, we have a life together. Powers come to me when I need them. Yaokun comes out and talks to me once in a while. The old man helps me out with anything that I might need. I have a family. In this world, my name is Yukita Jon, but in another world, they call me the… "Unborn Demon Slayer." There are more worlds than just ours. Monsters, demons, and unique people like me, who visit from that world to ours. My story has not been finished… it has only begun.

Printed in the United States
By Bookmasters